Written by Claudia Blood
Cover design by Sunset Rose Books

Copyright 2021 by Claudia Blood

Paperback ISBN: 978-1-954603-44-8

All rights reserved.

No part of this book may be reproduced in any form or by any electronic or mechanical means, including information storage and retrieval systems, without written permission from the author, except for the use of brief quotations in a book review.

This book is licensed for your personal enjoyment only. This is a work of fiction. All characters and events portrayed in this book are fictional, and any resemblance to real people or incidents is purely coincidental.

Seriously, I make stuff up all the time. It's my job.

Claudia Blood acknowledges that all of her writing is 100% her own. No part of it is created by generative Artificial Intelligence (AI) software of any kind. Yes, that means that it's sometimes flawed, but she's okay with that.

❀ Created with Vellum

MARKED

VALERIA'S ORIGIN STORY

THE MERGED SERIES

CLAUDIA BLOOD

DRAGON BANE PUBLISHING

ABOUT MARKED

**Searching for her lost sister, she uncovers a terrible secret—
one that could cost her everything...**

Valeria uncovers a dark secret that could save her and reunite
her with the one she loves. But she soon realizes that the
demons she's up against will stop at nothing to keep her from
finding the truth.

Set in a world where ancient family secrets hold immense
power, Marked is a heart-pounding standalone Novelette in the
Merged Series.

With her loved ones under the control of ruthless enemies,
Valeria must navigate a treacherous family feud that could
ultimately cost her everything.

Read if you you love intense family dynamics, huge family
secrets, and gripping action.

This is the origin story for Valeria. Find out how she got her
tattoos.

Trigger warning:
This book contains demon possession, death, flashback to child
abuse, and one small torture scene.

1

VALERIA

<u>Dawn, Sprout fifth, 298 years post-Merge</u>

Valeria dreamed of spiders. Six large black spiders rested on a red-sheened web. Three silver moths struggled on the sticky center. With a twist, one moth escaped and fluttered away.

The other two, more deeply cocooned in the web, struggled valiantly but couldn't follow. The largest spider reared on its hind legs and thrummed the nearest threads. The five smaller spiders did the same until the moths shook with the vibrations.

Valeria woke to a high-pitched hum in her head. The mental family network, her psychic connection to the family buzzed with anger. She'd never felt this much anger. Anger was normal, but not this level of rage. She shivered. The only way to get information was to enter the network more fully. Dread closed her throat. Going into the network brought the whole family's awareness on her. If they wanted to, they could read her thoughts and witness her failures.

After three deep breaths to clear her mind, she entered the network. Her grandmother's and aunts' black presences and Winifred's dark silver one shone, but Corona's pale silver was gone. Not weak, not distant, but snuffed out as if it had never been. Even in sleep, the family's presence stayed in the network. Corona's absence could only mean one thing: She was dead.

Valeria blinked her eyes, pushed the connection to the back of her mind, and focused instead on her room. It had been their room years ago. Faint moonlight shone from the window highlighting Corona's old bed, stripped to a bare mattress. The room shimmered with Valeria's next blink. Maybe she could cast a spell to remove the lost lonely feeling that ached inside her chest. On the floor, the spell circle's white chalk sparkled in the light, but it gave her no ideas. She closed her eyes and let the tears fall for just a moment. Corona couldn't be dead. She was so young, a few years younger than Valeria. Corona was gone and it was her fault. If only...

What felt like a thousand tiny hooks embedded in her ribs pulled at her chest. Only Isabella, her grandmother, could use the network to compel a witch to come to her. Why was she being called? She couldn't control the magic within her, so she wasn't eligible to become a full witch. Still, the pull dragged her out of bed, with just enough time to grab a robe and slippers. Then it pulled her down the cobbled pathway from the inner-city mansions, to the twisted remains of old town.

Her hastily donned robe fluttered in the cold breeze. A shiver lodged at the back of her neck. Valeria rubbed at it, trying to dispel the feeling of being watched. The feeling deepened, causing her to peer at the passing buildings. If she saw whomever it was, maybe she could avoid confrontation.

A shadow detached itself from an alley ahead.

"Where you off to, Miss?" The man was nothing but sinew and skin wrapped around sharp bones. No teeth poked out from his mouth as he spoke. Wide, dilated eyes watched her. The faint smell of turpentine surrounded him.

"Stay away from me," Valeria snapped. Fear rippled in her belly and she backed away. She could control this. She had to. She had to control her magic's response to danger.

She backed into something hard and warm. Her heart plummeted and she turned to see what it was. A taller heavier version of the first man grabbed her shoulder. The smell of turpentine was stronger as he chuckled.

"Let go!" Valeria tried to pry his fingers off.

Her vision swirled and a sound like a swarm of black flies engulfed her. The man let go of her shoulder and fell back. He stared for a moment, his mouth gaping, until the swirling black cloud around her head rushed into his mouth. Then he began to wail, which made her toes clench.

"No, stop," she moaned. "Not again!"

Valeria stumbled away as he continued to scream and thrash. She gagged when his body liquefied and the bones collapsed inside the skin with a wet plop. The black cloud absorbed the liquid and left a desiccated husk. The cloud dove back into her mouth. Valeria swallowed back bile and gagged on the taste of rotten fish until it cleared her throat. She slowly turned to face the first man. If she didn't get him away, her magic might decide to kill him as well.

"You next?" She lifted her eyebrow, hoping he did not notice her shaking hands.

He yelped and fled back to the alley.

The black cloud she'd swallowed ate at her stomach. The burning sensation was getting worse. Her magic had escaped her control and harmed another. She darted a glance at the remains and swallowed convulsively. It couldn't continue; she had to do something to stop it. If she couldn't control herself then she'd end it. She'd cut the ties to magic or cut her own life. Whatever it took.

She only had a heartbeat before the insistent tug resumed with enough force to bend her ribs.

It led her to an intact two-story building in the very center of old town. The other gutted buildings leaned away from its faint red glow. The door opened before she could touch it. She followed the pull down the stairs to the basement. Even though she'd never been here before, she knew it was where the family had first discovered their magic. First blood rites and other sacred ceremonies happened here. Could this mean despite her lack of control, they might make her a full witch? Hope lightened her step. Maybe if she became a full witch and was accepted, she would get the key that would allow her to control her magic.

The pull in her ribs disappeared once she entered the room. Candles flickered on the walls of the small stone room. Six witches stood in a semi-circle, shoulder to shoulder. They were clothed in red blouses with fitted bodices decorated with embroidered roses and heavy, green velour skirts. They appraised her with cold, dark eyes. Eyes filled with dislike and judgement. Any hope of being welcomed to the coven as a full member died with how they looked at her. Like she'd gravely disappointed them. First blood rites had to be earned. This must be something else. Two aunts grabbed her arms and pulled her into their circle.

Valeria smiled at her cousin, but Winifred turned away with a sniff. Winifred was paler than the last time Valeria had seen her. Neither of them were full witches. It was odd that they'd both be here. There must be very significant family news. The anger from the family network meant the news wouldn't be good. She knew her family didn't mourn as other families did, so the news was probably not about Corona's death.

The circle parted as her, grandmother, Isabella stepped into its center. With flawless pale skin, deep red lips, and dark red eyes, she looked like a model, but something in her expression said she was more predator than lamb. She tossed her long black braid from one shoulder to the other. "It is as I feared. Corona is lost to us." She rotated slowly to face each witch in turn.

"What happened?" Aunt Paula was the oldest of the aunts and had the highest rank behind Isabella. She was the only one brave enough to question Isabella.

"The breeder mate and his family took her from us." Isabella's gaze lingered on Winifred and Valeria and then went back to Aunt Paula. "Her soul was ripped right out of her body."

Valeria's ears rang and she felt as if a giant hand had slapped her.

"That's possible?" Winifred asked, sounding just as stunned as Valeria felt.

"We are immune to this attack if first blood rites are performed," Isabella said.

The aunts murmured and glanced at each other, but they avoided looking at Valeria and Winifred. Valeria couldn't quite catch her breath. How could a soul be ripped from a body? What sort of evil monster had Corona ended up mating?

"We must seek vengeance for Corona," Isabella said. "And we must protect our own."

She examined Winifred and Valeria with pursed lips. "Winifred, you should be the one to seek vengeance. This will be your first blood rite. You are closer to becoming one of us."

Valeria's heart rebelled. All of her sorrow and loneliness concentrated in this moment. She needed to be the one to seek vengeance. It was the only way to get closure and prove herself ready. "No, Grandmother." Valeria stepped forward. "I should be the one."

"You?" Isabella sneered. "You are not ready to join us."

Isabella's glance snapped with magical power, pushing Valeria back into the circle.

"Winifred..." Isabella continued.

Frustration boiled over, making Valeria reckless. Maybe standing up to her Grandmother would show that she was ready. "No." Valeria stepped forward again. "Vengeance is mine."

"You dare question my orders?" Isabella growled at the end of her question. "You can't even control your own body."

Valeria clasped her hands to hide their tremors. It didn't matter how scared she was. This was her one chance to prove herself and earn a place in the coven. Her one chance to avenge her sister's death. "It is my right as Corona's blood sister."

Her aunts laughed, evil, wild laughter that brought down the temperature in the room.

The candles flickered low. Their faces merged with the shadows and Valeria could see only their faintly glowing red eyes. Isabella's were the brightest. Winifred, who was not in the shadows, watched with her bottom lip caught between her teeth.

"Begone. You are not strong enough to be here." Isabella raised her hands, palms towards Valeria, and pushed with her magic. Valeria slid back and out the door which slammed in her face.

The handle turned, but as hard as she pushed the door, it wouldn't open. Futile rage bubbled to her heart, making it beat wildly. She focused her energy on kicking the door. She screamed at the door, ramming her shoulder into it, until her shoulder ached and she was covered in sweat.

It hadn't budged.

Valeria put her forehead on the door and breathed until she caught her breath. "I swear I will find Corona's killers myself and bring them to justice," she whispered.

2

———

VALERIA

<u>Mid-morning, Sprout fifth, 298 years post-Merge</u>

Valeria raced back to her room, barely noticing the city as she went. If she was going to find Corona's killer before the Family did, she would have to act fast. She noted the time on the grandfather clock.

Valeria sat in her meditation circle. As part of her training, she had once been bullied into biting a brightly colored caterpillar. Even that stomach turning experience hadn't prepared her for the foul taste that entered her mouth when she called her magical power. Dread formed a knot blocking her magic. *Why must magic be so foul?*

She breathed in working on the internal knot. Finding Corona's killer was important to her. Worth the cost her magic demanded. When the knot dissolved, she gathered her will, and called to her magic. The black energy coursed up her skin and clouded her vision for a moment and then formed a small globe which hung above her.

She heaved thick green bile in the pot she had positioned in her circle. When the nausea faded, she shaped the energy into a questing spell. It was like packing a snowball made of thorns as her hands pressed the power into a prickly ball.

The black energy rotated in front of her right at eye level. The ball seemed to be taunting her. "What now?" it seemed to ask.

Valeria steeled her will, directing the magic as she spoke her command. "Find Corona's breeder mate."

The magic should've sped off in the direction of the Breeder, but instead it continued to rotate, ignoring her.

"Find Corona's body," she said.

Still nothing. Dismay shook her control and the ball wobbled in the air. She needed to do something with the called magic soon, or it would attack her.

She glanced at the clock. It had been over an hour since she'd left the witches, more than enough time for the coven to find the breeder. Had they? She pulled her ear. Isabella would know, but she wouldn't be pleased to be spied upon, but what choice did Valeria have? She could feel the magic she'd called growing restless.

"Find Isabella," she commanded.

The ball turned into an arrow and sped off. Valeria left her physical form behind and followed it with her spirit. She found the coven still in the basement. A loose shield of black energy swirled around them. Valeria dodged around it to get close enough to see what they were doing.

The five women in the circle chanted as they held hands and walked slowly in a circle. Isabella held an ornately carved knife that looked like a skull with a single tooth as the blade. The blade dripped blood on a prone body that was tied, gagged, and blindfolded. Magic pulsed and shimmered around the body obscuring who it was.

Could they have found the breeder so quickly?

Isabella plunged the knife's tip into her captive's back leaving a glowing line. The body bucked and writhed in agony and then turned towards Valeria.

The magic shimmer cleared for a moment revealing Winifred.

Valeria gasped, confusion, and revulsion crashed into her.

Isabella paused mid cut, her eyes glowing. "I see you."

With a scooping motion of her hand, Isabella threw Valeria back to her body. Landing with a thud, Valeria sprawled on her back, ruining the chalk lines, and breaking her casting circle.

Her heart raced as wildly as if she had just run the whole way back from old town. She tried to stand, but she shook too badly. One of the fallen candles lit a paper on the floor on fire. Crawling over, she dumped the pot on it. Rancid smoke filled the room. The smoke brought tears to her eyes and burned her throat. She coughed and crawled out the door, still too weak to stand.

Valeria slumped to the ground, closed her eyes, and breathed deeply until the tremors passed. What had she just witnessed? Was this part of the first blood rites? What a horrible ordeal, but it must be worth the pain to become a full member of the coven. It had to mean the coven hadn't found Corona's killer. That meant she had more time to find him herself. But how? The questing spell had failed. She wasn't sure if it was her magical control or something else that had prevented the spell from working. She needed more information.

Ten minutes later, back in her room with the windows thrown open, Valeria washed the chalk from the ruined spell circle and re-chalked it. A perfect circle and then one triangle within and then a second triangle upside down from the first.

She placed six silver candles for her future position as a sixth level witch where the triangles touched the circle. That level was the most powerful level of witchery. Poor Corona hadn't even made it out of the breeding pool to the first level. They'd said she'd been born with something missing. Her inner spirit had been weak.

Valeria pulled a wooden box from under her bed and opened it. Six silk-covered objects tied with silver cord nestled in the box. Each package contained a personal object which she would place in each inner triangle to strengthen the circle.

Valeria lifted each item and kissed the bow before untying it. She unwrapped the silk to reveal each item.

The silver necklace from her mother who had died giving birth to her third sister.

A blue, silk-covered button she had salvaged from Corona's favorite dress.

A grey and gold stone that had sparkled and called to her one day when she was a young girl in the garden.

A dried red rose that somehow kept its beauty.

A tangled ball of purple yarn. She wasn't sure why she had chosen it, but it felt right.

Lastly, she replaced the scrubbed pot back in position for the next casting.

How was she going to find Corona's killers? Was it really the breeder mate Corona had married? What had Isabella been doing with Winifred? How much time did she have before Isabella made her regret spying?

The circle completed, she closed her eyes and went into a trance.

Her mind drifted to an image of Corona. Corona had squealed as she pulled Valeria along the dark hallway away from their bedroom towards the front room. The heavy carpet had muffled their passage.

"Come on." Corona sang softly to some silly made-up

rhythm while hopping on one foot. "Come see what I discovered."

"Please," Valeria whispered. "We're not allowed to leave the bed until full light."

"You have to see this." Corona giggled with child-like abandon. Strands of dark hair escaped from her sleeping braid.

"Isabella will beat us or worse." Valeria glanced behind them.

"Only if she catches us," Corona sang.

"She always catches us," Valeria muttered, but she followed anyway.

"Come on, Valeria, you won't believe your eyes." For some reason this made Corona laugh. "Watch."

Corona stopped in front of the only mirror in the house. A pair of carved serpents encircled the glass with entwined tails at the bottom and mouths gaping at each other at the top of the mirror. The witches brought visitors to sit by this mirror. Mirrors revealed the true selves of those that sat before them.

Corona vibrated with barely contained energy. "Can you feel it?"

She could feel something faintly. She could breathe easier and it felt like a weight that had pressed her down had vanished.

Valeria shook her head and compared herself to Corona in the mirror. Same height. Same dark hair. A swath of freckles sprinkled over the bridge of Corona's upturned nose. While Corona struggled to restrain herself from grinning, Valeria frowned. Everything about Valeria was straight and serious. Everything about Corona was round and cheerful.

Then for just a moment, Valeria's eyes turned bright blue before slowly changing to their normal smokey topaz color.

Valeria glanced at Corona in the mirror. Corona also had blue eyes and they stayed blue for far longer than Valeria's had before they changed to the same topaz.

When the last of the blue had faded, the whole room seemed to darken.

"What does it mean?" Valeria stared, looking for any hint that the blue still existed.

"I don't know," Corona whispered. She shook her head. "Did you feel it?"

"Yes." Valeria knew that if anyone were to find out about this, they would both be punished. In fact, they might be kicked out of the family. Valeria leaned toward Corona. "You must never tell another about this."

"But?" Corona's brows furrowed.

"Promise me."

"If it is that important to you, I promise." Corona shrugged.

Valeria sighed, sagging against the wall. When she looked up, the dark figure of Isabella stood near the door. Valeria felt the blood drain from her face and felt a rip of dread. Caught. They were caught. How much had Isabella seen? How much had she heard?

"What are you doing?" Isabella demanded.

"N-n-nothing." Valeria stepped forward to block Corona, but Isabella's hand touched Valeria between the eyes. Valeria felt as if she had stepped into a fire; pain radiated from her forehead to the bottom of her feet. Tears trickled down her cheek and she bit her lip to keep from screaming. The world spun. She staggered back against the wall.

"What will I do with you?" Isabella brushed past Valeria and grabbed Corona's arm.

Isabella's eyes narrowed, and she clenched her other hand into a fist. Corona fell to her knees choking. "Not even good enough for the first level. Perhaps another beating?"

Valeria pushed past the pain, she had to. Corona had barely survived the last beating. "P-Perhaps a breeder? Since she is so useless at magic. We have no other active breeders."

Valeria grasped her hands together behind her back, finger-nails digging into her own flesh.

Corona continued to make choking sounds.

Valeria kept her breath even and looked at the floor. She couldn't look at her sister lest she betray how much she cared. Isabella would use any sign of weakness and exploit it. Perhaps killing Corona as a lesson to Valeria.

Finally, Isabella snapped her fingers. Corona collapsed on the floor with a wheeze.

"Valeria, get back in bed," Isabella said.

Valeria shot a glance toward them as she scrambled to obey. For just a moment in the mirror, Isabella had looked far older, with a bald head and dark circles under her eyes. Then Isabella dragged Corona out of the room, and out of Valeria's life.

Isabella's face had looked the same then as it did in the basement circle when they'd laughed at her.

What were the spirits trying to tell her? Why that scene? It had been years ago and was her last memory of Corona before she had left to prepare to be bred. Valeria blinked back tears. It was her last memory of Corona alive and the last time her magic had behaved.

She remembered how over the years, after long days of lessons, she would get up early the next morning and look in the mirror. Sometimes she could swear that Corona was just behind her, laughing. She could feel her sister as if she were in the same room. It wasn't the faint presence on the family network, but something closer to who Corona really had been. Valeria had finally smuggled her own mirror into the house so she didn't have to leave her room to see it.

Valeria rubbed her eyes. The first traces of dawn lightened the sky.

Dawn! Was that the message? She needed to seek Corona at

dawn when she had felt the closest to Corona. Excitement and hope lightened her chest.

Valeria lit the candles. There wouldn't be much time before dawn. At the last moment, she rose, grabbed her hand mirror, and set it so she could see her own eyes. When the first hint of blue surfaced, she called her magic. At first, nothing happened. Then she heard the faint tinkling of bells coming closer and closer until they stopped and the smell of cinnamon and freshly baked bread replaced it. Smells that were wholesome and good.

A golden pool of magic coalesced in a ball at eye level and spun in the air in front of her. She gaped for almost a full minute at the golden sphere and then grinned. It had been effortless and had left her feeling good. She knew dawn was a time of rebirth and renewal, but wasn't sure why her magic would behave so differently now.

"Find Corona," Valeria said.

The orb changed into an arrow and darted off. Her spirit followed, but as soon as she couldn't see her eyes in the mirror, the arrow faded.

This hadn't happened before. Maybe she needed to be able to see herself in the mirror for this new magic to work.

She recalled the magic and when it sped off, she stretched her spirit to follow the ball, but kept enough tethered in her body that she could still see the mirror. This was harder than anything else she'd done. She fought for control and her eyes remained blue.

The arrow hovered near a manor house just outside of town.

The image shimmered as the spirit piece tethered to her body loosened. No, just a little longer she begged. A bead of sweat dropped to her nose and hung on the very tip. A storm cloud of black energy coalesced and pooled around her head. Where had the black magic come from?

The golden arrow darted forward into the house. A formal

staircase dominated the front room. On the far wall hung a picture of Corona and a man who had to have been her husband.

The black magic around Valeria's head, struck at her spirit tether point like an angry snake. Instinctively she pulled her spirit back, slapping away the black energy until her full spirit lodged back in her body. Her eyes, still fixed on the hand mirror, reverted to topaz as the black energy coursed down her throat. Dread filled her gut like some large, moving snake. She dry heaved into the pot, unable to get rid of the taste of rotten fish.

It had been worth it. She'd found the house Corona had been in. She stood on shaky legs and gathered a traveling pouch and her small collection of personal effects. She needed to get out of this house and find that manor house.

Then in a startling moment of foresight she knew once she left this house, she was never coming back.

An hour later, Valeria sat on the snow-covered rooftop of a small shed across from the manor the magic had shown her. It was the only place that allowed her to see into the house and still be somewhat protected from view.

The lightly falling snow left tiny droplets of water on her bare arms. She sat next to the chimney with her hands braced behind her. The snow melted, leaving a bare patch around her. Across the yard, a lazy spiral of smoke drifted up from the chimney.

She had no idea how she was going to get vengeance. She could purposely let her magic out and let it harm the breeder who had hurt Corona, but her stomach rolled at the idea. That would be a horrible thing to do. It was bad enough it happened when her power escaped her control, but to do it purposely seemed wrong. If she could look inside the manor to see what she was up against before making a plan.

With a shake, she left her body and entered the window. The

room held a large portrait of her sister with her husband. Valeria studied the oil painting. He didn't look like a killer. The artist had caught him looking at Corona with a half-smile, his hand clasping hers to his chest. A wide grin lit Corona's face. She looked happy.

Valeria drifted around the room and then made her way down the hall, poking her head into each room. A study and yet another bedroom, all looked empty.

Golden power fluttered in the air around the last door off the hallway like a muslin curtain in an open window on a gusty spring day.

Valeria drifted closer. What could produce such power? She tugged at her lower lip, then shrugged and went through the door.

The wind shifted within the power and pulled her toward its center. She turned to flee, but it held on dragging her until she pressed against something solid.

The material world shouldn't effect her spirit. Yet Valeria was stuck. She bucked and struggled, but was trapped.

The power pulsed, ripping away her stored power. Then the pulsing stopped, and she was able to push herself away from the wall. She fled back to her body without a backward glance.

She woke up shivering and covered in snow. Her teeth chattered as she slowly stood and looked around. Something was wrong. Witches in her family didn't get cold. She hadn't been cold when she'd explored the house with her spirit.

She jumped up and down in place, rubbing her arms. As she moved more vigorously her foot slipped and she slid off the roof and landed in a pile of snow.

For a moment, she looked up at the sky before scrambling out of the snowbank. Her simple dress clung to her body and legs. She was freezing and would freeze to death if she didn't seek shelter. She was too far away from other houses to reach them in her current state. Her first priority was to get warm. She hobbled to the front door of the manor house and knocked. Maybe a house servant would let her in. The wind stirred up goose bumps and her teeth chattered.

Corona's husband answered the door. He choked when he saw her, his gaze darting behind her.

"How did you find us?" he demanded. He pushed his arm back, forcing the person behind him farther away.

She caught sight of the dark-haired woman. Valeria rubbed her eyes and looked again. Could it be? "C-c-co-orona?"

With a wave of his hand, Valeria flew back into the snow.

3

VALERIA

<u>Afternoon, Sprout fifth, 298 years post-Merge</u>

Valeria opened her eyes to a pink canopy above her head. She felt strangely at peace. A pop turned her gaze to the fireplace. Did they really have canopies and glowing fires in the grate in the afterlife? She moved her gaze around the room wondering where she was.

Pastel flowers decorated the wall. Everything looked cheerful, perhaps even child-like. It was so different from the room she'd grown up in. She didn't belong here, and she needed to leave before something terrible happened.

She kicked off the blanket and sat up. As her feet touched the floor, she noticed Corona sitting on the rocking chair next to the bed. Her dark hair neatly pinned in a bun made Valeria think of the schoolteachers other kids learned from.

"I must be dead." Valeria smiled. "Sorry I got you killed."

"What are you talking about?" Corona grinned and rocked the chair. "We are not dead."

"But it's m-my fault you…" Valeria looked away from Corona. She struggled with the guilt from that day all those years ago. If she would have stopped Corona from going to the mirror room that morning, she never would have been sent to be a breeder.

Corona turned Valeria's chin. "Oh, Valeria, I know it may be hard to understand, but I am ever so glad I became a breeder." She seemed sincere. She leaned forward and held Valeria's gaze.

"Why can't I feel you? Why do I feel…" Valeria stopped mid-sentence and furrowed her brow. The family network was gone. She felt none of the family. A strange combination of fear and hope lodged in her throat. She wasn't sure if she was going to laugh or cry.

"Free?" Corona laughed gaily, fanning herself with her hand. "Tell me you feel light and free."

Valeria closed her eyes for a moment and just allowed the feeling to float within her. She hadn't realized until it was gone that the network had felt like a trap. She wasn't sure what to think. Corona was alive when the family had said she was dead. The family network that had been her constant companion since childhood was gone. She didn't know if she was still a witch without the network. None of it made any sense. She was adrift in confusion. Everything she had thought she knew was a lie.

"Come on, I need to show you something." Corona's voice was gentle and coaxing as if she knew what Valeria was feeling at this moment. She stood and took Valeria's hand. "It is just down the hallway."

"What?"

"It is hard to explain. It would be better if I showed you, come on." Corona tugged Valeria down the hall.

Pictures of Corona's husband's family watched their progress until they came to a door with a sun carved in the wood. Corona touched the door and it swung open silently. The comforting milky warmth of vanilla surrounded them. The scent meant the room was protected.

"I promise this room holds answers to your questions." Corona tugged Valeria into the room.

In the middle of the room stood a large globe. A dark shape swirled beneath its translucent surface. Some aquatic leviathan with large sharp teeth and gaping maw circled inside. Hands with long claws swiped at the globe as it sought purchase.

"I don't understand." Valeria walked closer. She put her hand on the outside of the globe. The being reoriented and pressed its face against the globe. Valeria's face, but softened like a wax candle being burned, peered back at her.

Valeria jumped back and blinked. "W-What is that?"

"It is you. Or more accurately something sharing your body. At least it had been."

"I-I-I. Was I cursed?" Confusion swirled within Valeria, making it hard to hear. This didn't seem to answer her questions it only added to the pile of questions circling her mind. She forced herself to focus on Corona.

"It's a long story, but it all started with Isabella," Corona said.

"Grandmother?" Valeria frowned.

"Actually, there are a couple greats before the grandmother part." Corona's soft blue dress swirled around Corona's ankles as she paced, arms gesturing. "Although, she was not so great. I know this will be hard for you to believe."

"But?" Valeria prompted.

"But, our family, beginning with Isabella made a pact with the devil, and demon spawn has possessed them." Corona turned and pointed. "That."

Valeria froze. "T-that was in me."

"That is what gave us the family network." Corona nodded. "An evil Valeria."

"And the power?" Valeria asked, thinking about the rolling black cloud of magic.

Corona shrugged. "Both the good Valeria and the evil Valeria have power."

Valeria sat in silence and then reached for Corona's hand. She needed to be connected with her sister. She needed that connection that had been there on the mornings Valeria had looked in the mirror. She realized now that she had felt Corona and more faintly Winifred on those mornings.

Winifred too must have a demon within her. Was that why she was being tortured?

"I defied Isabella to avenge you. They were doing something to Winifred. I couldn't help her." Valeria couldn't meet Corona's gaze.

"You can't help that now." Corona embraced Valeria and held her close. "We have to focus on you. Once the demon is removed, you have twenty-four hours to make it permanent." Corona released Valeria and stepped back.

A mixture of betrayal and shock stole her breath. It was bad enough that Isabella had put a demon inside her, but to have such a short time to defeat it seemed unfair. "How?" Valeria looked over at the globe. The distorted face watched her.

"Only the one it occupied has the ability to destroy it," Corona said it as if her words were a part of a bigger ritual. Who had coached her? "It becomes a battle of wits and power."

"How am I supposed to defeat that?" Valeria pointed at the leering face in the globe.

"It is within you to know how to defeat your demon," Corona said.

"How do you know? Did someone help you?" Valeria asked.

Corona hesitated and then bit her lip. "I can't tell you more until you defeat it."

"What if I can't defeat it?" She hadn't been able to control her power before, that may not have changed. The feeling of being in over her head had her head pounding. She'd spent the years since being separated from Corona at the mercy of that demon. She hadn't been able to control it then, what made her think that she could now?

Corona interrupted her thoughts by handing Valeria a mirror. "Look at yourself. You have to truly believe you are free."

Valeria glanced at the mirror and when she saw her blue eyes, froze. Her eyes were no longer topaz. That could mean that the dawn magic was her magic. She'd only used that magic once, but it had worked about the same as the dark magic, but with no pain, no dread. She started to cough, which turned into a laugh. She couldn't stop laughing, and she gasped for breath.

"Breathe." Corona rubbed her back. "Just breathe."

"How is that..." Valeria trailed off with a frown and shake of her head.

"How is this lovely, joyful creature the same person you have seen in the mirror all these years?" Corona took her hand again. "This is what we would have been like had the demon not been feeding on our energy all this time."

Valeria shut her eyes and took a moment to take stock of her magic. When she reached for power the faint tinkling of bells and the smell of fresh bread heralded the golden energy coursing within her. The rotten fish smell was gone. Maybe she did have a chance. She had her magic. Of course, the demon had its own.

"Tell me everything you know," Valeria said. "I want this demon gone for good. You said twenty-four hours."

"Yes, well." Corona fiddled with her skirt, and for the first time she didn't meet Valeria's gaze. "You slept some of it away."

"How much is left?" Valeria braced herself for Corona's answer.

"Something just less than two hours," Corona said, sounding meek.

Valeria closed her eyes and rubbed her temples with her pointer fingers to keep the budding panic at bay. "I have two hours to prepare? Why did you let me sleep so long?"

"It was not my choice." Corona grimaced and twisted her fingers. "Removing the demon stripped your power."

"And sleep is the best way to recharge," Valeria finished with a sigh. If she'd been woken up early, she would have had no personal power. All the knowledge in the world wouldn't help her if she had nothing to fight with.

They sat in silence for a moment before a flash of worry lit upon Corona's face. "I forgot to ask… They, I mean, I need to know how you found me."

"Magic," Valeria wiggled her brows.

Corona's eyes widened and a hand went up to hover in front of her mouth. "Y-y-you worked magic to find me? But they said…"

"Dawn magic. I used a golden orb of magic and I didn't even get sick." Valeria grinned. "Something blocked the normal magic." She realized now that something about the dawn must've blocked the demon's magic. Or maybe the demon's hold on her.

Corona breathed again. "Oh, good. Then William did block us from demon scrying."

"How did you defeat yours?" Valeria asked, nodding toward the globe where the demon circled.

"You are better off not knowing," Corona said. "It will distract you from finding your own solution."

Valeria could only nod. Corona might not want to talk about it in case the demon won and escaped.

If Valeria had more time, she could research and learn everything there was to know about demons. As it was, she'd just have to do the best with what she had, the golden magic, that didn't seem to make her sick.

"The glass weakens as time gets closer. We are going to seal you in this room." She raised her hand before Valeria could protest. "Everything you need to defeat it is within you."

"How will you know if I am successful?"

"Oh, my sister." Corona hugged her close. "I will know."

With a final hug, Corona walked out of the room. The bolt shot into place and a sound like the light patter of rain came as the magic ward surrounded the room. Clock chimes echoed through the room. She would finish this one way or another in a couple – actually less than two short hours.

4

VALERIA

<u>Afternoon, Sprout fifth, 298 years post-Merge</u>

Valeria turned back to the globe to witness the first crash of the demon against the glass. Its nose squished into its face, pushing its eyes wider as it rammed its head into the glass sides of the globe over and over again. Claws scrabbled and squealed. It opened its mouth and rammed serrated teeth against the barrier, sounding like a pick digging a grave in rock.

She set up a quick circle. It wouldn't accord much protection, but she needed anything she could get. She still wasn't sure what she needed to do to defeat the demon.

The sound of the crashing changed and then the glass shattered. A triumphant roar shook the room. Valeria, even with her eyes closed, could smell damp rotten fish. She opened her eyes. Her own shadow stood before her, but it was a twisted and darker impression of her, with red eyes and a large mouth filled with jagged teeth. Valeria waited to see what it would do. It grinned even wider showing more of its teeth.

"Give up?" the thing croaked. "I look forward to having that body to myself from now on." It glanced at the clock. "All I have to do is wait. You are not strong enough to defeat me."

The minutes ticked by as Valeria realized the demon could be right. She had no idea what to do.

The shadow's eyes widened and then it disappeared.

Valeria stood in shock. "No."

She used her magical sight to scan the room, but it was empty of demon essence. It had left her alone in the warded room. The chime sounded on the clock. Time was running out.

Valeria created a seeking spell, immersing herself in the rush of bells and cinnamon.

"Show me my shadow."

The golden light shot away and Valeria followed it. It led back to the witches' basement. She entered, bracing herself for what she might see.

Winifred's naked body shook with each breath; columns of black symbols from the ancient language of the spells covered her skin. The black symbols were curses. Her translucent soul hovered partially out of her body with a nimbus of gold sparkles. Her feet radiated black. First blood ceremony must be how the demon took over. Revulsion twisted Valeria's insides. Another lie.

The aunts' crumpled human shells lay in a circle around Winifred. Above five black shadows with red eyes flew in circles, like crows around roadkill. Isabella paced in a circle in her own body. Her face was not much different from the demon shadows' faces. How had Valeria never recognized how evil Isabella was?

"Begone." One demon extended her claws and raked them across Winifred's spirit. The spirit shuddered and slipped further out of her body. More black ink filled in on the partial "envy" symbol on the curses on her skin. The next demon shadow took its turn attacking and adding ink to a symbol.

"What have we here?" Isabella turned to Valeria.

The rest of the demons turned and stared, including Winifred's spirit who said. "Look out behind you."

Valeria turned in time to see her evil twin barreling down on her.

"P-p-protect." A warding spell shimmered around Valeria, but it shattered under the black claws of her evil twin. Valeria screamed when the claws dug into her. A long strip of spirit and power ripped from her and coalesced into a golden blob. Her evil twin backed away, laughing, and popped the golden blob in her mouth.

Her evil twin disappeared in the shadows. Her aunts were no longer visible. It was weird that they no longer hovered.

This might be her only chance to help Winifred. Valeria went to Winifred who was still prone on the ground. "My God, what have they done?"

Winifred's eyes flickered open again. The topaz color of her eyes had more red in them. The demons were winning. She had to do something or the demon would take over.

"Let me heal you," Valeria said.

At Winifred's nod, Valeria reached forward to place her hand on Winifred's shoulder. Heat burned Valeria's hand and she jerked back with a hiss. "The pattern." She nodded toward the symbols tattooed on Winifred's body. "I am barred from touching you."

"My body burns my spirit now." Winifred's voice sounded calm and her gaze was direct and didn't mask the pain she was in. "I can't fight it much longer."

Anguish tightened her hands, digging her nails into her palms. "What can I do?"

"You need to destroy my body." Winifred took a shallow breath. The black around her feet throbbed.

"I..." Valeria shook her head. She couldn't do it. She couldn't kill her own cousin. There had to be a different way.

"I don't want it used for what they intend." Winifred winced and then said more quietly, "I can no longer stay in it. I'm sorry. But, maybe I can help you."

"No," Valeria said, "save your energy. There must be a way."

"You were always the strong one."

Winifred's soul bubbled from her heart, forming a cloud as it pulled away from her body. Winifred clapped her hands together and muttered, "Bildu konpresa."

The golden glow gathered in her hands as the rest of her body darkened. She pushed her hands out towards Valeria. "Go."

The power coiled and struck, hitting Valeria in the chest, and sinking in. Valeria flickered wildly, but used her training to accept the power instead of trying to resist the invasion.

"Destroy my body past resurrection." Winifred stared until Valeria gained enough control to nod.

Winifred's spirit released its hold on her body and spiraled up.

Valeria held out her hand palm up and focused on the sound of the bells until it felt like she was inside a giant church bell. A small gold pinpoint of light expanded out with each toll until the whole room was ablaze with light.

When Isabella and the aunts shrieked, Valeria pointed her finger at Winifred. Valeria stared at Winifred's peaceful form. Whatever part of Winifred she could have been friends with was gone, but still she hesitated. This was the daughter of her mother's sister. An early childhood friend. She would be lost forever. Valeria had no choice, she had to destroy Winifred's body. It was the right thing to do.

Valeria stared for one more moment and then lifted her hands to propel her magic toward Winifred. "Burn."

Winifred's body burst into flame. The tattoos disappeared into her blackening skin. Each dark hair lit at the end and burned back like a long drag on a cigarette. Then all that was left was an ash impression. After a moment, the ash drifted away.

Valeria closed her eyes and then fled back to her body.

It was no longer lying where she had left it. It stood smirking at her with bright red eyes. Valeria tried pushing her way back in, but was rebuffed and pushed back across the room. That's why her aunts had backed away from Winifred. They had been distracting Valeria so Valeria's evil twin could take over her body. The demon Corona had removed from Valeria's body, now had control of the body they had shared.

The demon snapped Valeria's soul anchor to her body. "All I have to do is hold you out for ten more minutes and your body becomes mine forever." It laughed and walked to the door of the room. "Corona!" It shouted in her voice, "I did it!"

"Valeria?" Corona's voice came through the door. "Is it really you?"

"Yes!" It laughed. Then it turned and smirked at Valeria as the door rattled and Corona shouted for the ward to be removed.

"No, Corona! Don't listen," Valeria shouted.

"You forgot you are outside your body, didn't you?" Evil Valeria laughed. "No body, no voice. Only I can hear you." It whispered so only Valeria could hear. "I want to make sure you see me punish your sister for her betrayal."

The ward dropped and the evil Valeria stood by the door arms raised, fingers spread. She looked like Valeria because she had taken over Valeria's physical form. Corona would be fooled and would die.

Fury and desperation twined within her spirit heart. She

leaped to the opening door and pushed it shut with a thrust of power. "No. Leave Corona out of this."

Evil Valeria cackled. "And what do you think you will do?"

Valeria thought about what she could do to save Corona. The evil Valeria would kill her and anyone else who had helped her escape. She needed a way to bar the evil Valeria from being able to touch Corona. Maybe she could expel the evil Valeria with the same trick the demon's had used on Winifred.

Valeria called her power, focusing on the cinnamon smell, until she looked through a haze of real cinnamon floating in the air. She flicked her fingers, embedding the spice as letters on evil Valeria's skin.

"What are you doing?" Evil Valeria hissed.

Valeria blasted her whole body until it was covered in blessing tattoos. When Valeria wrote the last symbol, evil Valeria's spirit shrieked and fled her body. A rolling thunder cloud of power formed above her body which slid to the floor. Now both Valeria and her evil twin were spirits and disconnected from her body. Without a spirit embedded inside, her physical shell would wither away and die.

"I will take you with me." Evil Valeria extended long glowing claws and ripped gashes in Valeria's soul. She bled golden power.

The door burst open. Corona ran into the room and wrapped her arms around Valeria's limp body. Corona pressed her forehead against Valeria's. "Don't be dead."

Evil Valeria screamed and dove towards Corona's back.

Valeria intercepted her evil twin and engulfed her, wrapping her spirit around her evil twin, and calling forth her power. She heard bells, smelled cinnamon, and then for just an instant–a memory of the sun shining and her jumping up from the arm of the rocking chair to the arms of her mother and looking up into her laughing face shot through her consciousness. Using the last of Winifred's extra power, Valeria formed a sphere around the demon and forced it smaller and smaller. The clock began to chime the witching hour.

"Nooooo."

With the last chime of the clock, the sphere forced the demon out of existence.

Valeria floated to where Corona rocked her dying body. It would be so easy to let go. To float away from it all and follow where Winifred had gone. Besides Corona, there was nothing here for Valeria. And Corona didn't need her. She'd found her own happiness.

A popping sound behind her, drew her attention away from Corona. A spirit eye formed looked around and disappeared.

Valeria's stomach dropped. The coven knew where Corona was. If Valeria left now, she'd leave Corona to face the coven with no warning. Valeria entered her own body and released the last of her power to repair her soul's connection.

Valeria opened her eyes. "Corona. You are in grave danger."

Not seeming to hear Valeria's words, Corona hugged her closer. "You did it."

Corona's husband, put a hand on Corona's shoulder and grinned broadly down at Valeria. "I can't believe you did it."

"They know where you are." Valeria whispered. "You must prepare for the full coven to attack."

"We need to know what we are up against. We have never been able to save two people from a family before," he said. "The demons tend to convert those they can and hide the weaker ones. Your demon was not a breeder like Corona's?"

"Not a breeder." Valeria struggled to think. "I would have been a witch in the sixth circle."

"Sixth circle?" He blinked. "Are you sure? That is the most powerful demon. We have only successfully removed breeder demons or first level demons where the human had a chance against the weak demon in them. Anything more and the human just doesn't have enough personal power."

"Where are my manners?" Corona said. "William this is Valeria; Valeria, William. I told you my sister could do it."

"I should never have doubted you, love." William grinned at Corona, but turned back to Valeria. "You have to tell me everything. Maybe there is something we can use to get more possessed witches free."

The phrase more possessed witches made Valeria think of Winifred. Valeria closed her eyes. "I couldn't have done it alone. Winifred helped me."

"What happened to Winifred?" Corona asked.

"I witnessed a first blood ceremony." Valeria shuddered. "It's how they take over the human body fully."

"This is just amazing," William said. "I need you to tell me everything you can. Let me get my notebook."

"Later." Valeria struggled against the tiredness. William and Corona didn't seem to understand the danger they were in and she was running out of energy. "Isabella knows where we are."

Valeria heard him asking more questions about first blood ceremony, but she didn't care. She had to rest. She'd tried three times to warn them. Hopefully they had good protections. But that was a worry for another day.

For the first time Valeria slept without a spider web in her dreams.

THE END

~

Congratulations on reaching the end of Valeria's origin story! Stay tuned for a sneak peek of the first chapter in the second book of the Merged Series: "Thorn of the Rose." Find out how Valeria uses her new powers.

Enjoy this book? You can make a big difference...

Reviews are the most powerful tools when it comes to getting notice for my books.

If you enjoyed this book, I'd be so grateful if you'd spend just five minutes leaving a review (as short as you like!).

Thank you very much.

BOOK 2: THORN OF THE ROSE

Excerpt from Chapter 1: Rose

Rose Callahand opened her eyes. The shield protecting the town of Hope glimmered like a soap bubble. She'd made it through. Relief filled her chest with warmth. Her mission still had a chance.

She didn't remember actually crossing the shield. Her last memory was touching the shield at high sun, but now the dew on the grass and the first hint of light made everything seem gray. Had it taken all afternoon and night to cross? She shivered. The trees loomed above her. Nothing moved. The silence weighed her down.

Mistress Yaneli had determined that the shield was corrupted and was the reason for the sicknesses running rampant through Hope. Rose's mission seemed simple: take the stone necklace with the fire symbol to the man who would be waiting for her outside of the shield. Giving him the stone would allow him to break the shield around Hope.

Rose got to her knees and touched her neck where the stone should be.

There was no necklace.

Panic added a beat to her heart. Had she lost it? She slapped at her pockets. Nothing. Without it, her mission was a failure and her girls were in danger. Fear and failure crept up her back. The panic doubled.

No, she couldn't have failed.

The silver stone had been on a piece of twine. Perhaps the twine had broken in the crossing. She scanned the ground near her and saw a glimmer of gold. A different necklace with a thin gold chain and a locket sat in the grass. It wasn't what she was looking for, but she picked it up anyway.

The necklace stung her finger. Pain radiated up her hand, making it clench on the chain. The pain passed after a moment, leaving her dizzy. Someone else must have lost this necklace; she could try to return it.

Rose put on the chain. A strong urge to open the locket tightened her fingers. She ran her fingertip along the seam. The urge she felt was unnatural in its strength. The mission was more important than what was inside the locket. She would look inside later after looking for the stone necklace.

She dropped the locket, and when it hit her chest, a sudden foreboding struck her along with the sense that once she opened the locket, she would never be able to put back what she released into the world. This was her Pandora's Box. She shook her head to dispel the feeling. The mission and her girls were more important.

As she searched more ground around her, she resisted the urge to look inside the locket. But the necklace warmed against her chest and pulled at her imagination. What would be within it? Could it help her find the stone and salvage her mission? Could it help her protect her girls from Mistress Yaneli?

The last thought brought her up short. There was much she

would risk, including this mission for Mistress Yaneli, to protect her daughters.

Finally, she opened the locket, revealing a photo of her two daughters grinning at the camera with their brown hair curling around their faces. She didn't remember taking such a picture. On the other side was engraved, "So we can see those we have lost". The dizziness returned, her chest burned, and she leaned heavily on one arm.

Suddenly, the knowledge that her daughters were dead hit her in the heart. *My girls are dead.* Loss, sadness, and regret throttled her heart, squeezing it until she couldn't breathe.

Hope had killed her girls. She was sure of that. The thought echoed in her head and fear rose from her burning chest. Overwhelming, crushing fear brought tears to her eyes and blurred the world. She had to get away from Hope and never go back.

Rose stumbled to her feet, gasping for breath. The smell of the loam with its hint of decayed leaves filled her nose.

Hope was behind her, so she scrambled forward.

She stumbled, landing hard against a tree. The bark was rough against her fingers. Her breath caught in her lungs, producing short, choppy sobs in her throat.

She pushed forward blindly, tripping over something, then she toppled. The ground rushed up to meet her. Dirt dusted her mouth and pain lanced her hands and knees. She had to keep moving. The desperate urge to distance herself from Hope spurred her forward.

Rose crawled.

The sound of her own breathing echoed in her ears. She crawled until the ground gave way in front of her, and she tumbled forward and landed hard. The fear loosened its hold on her chest, but it still stalked too close.

She took a pull of cool air and worked to calm herself.

A crunch sounded next to her. She opened her eyes to a pair

of boots. Crouched next to her was a young man with scars covering his face. The man tilted his head, evaluating her with eyes that seemed far older than his young appearance. "Are you okay?"

She nodded even though she wasn't sure if it was true. The fear was still there in the back of her mind. It was smaller and more manageable. But the sense of grief from losing her girls still weighed her down. She tucked the necklace under her shirt and tried to focus on survival. She couldn't go back to Hope. Even thinking the town's name brought the fear closer.

"Need help standing?" His gaze traveled from her skinned knees to her nose and eyes. His scarred face twisted with sympathy. He had the look of a man who was distressed by a crying woman.

"At some point." She lifted her chin even as the tears fell down her cheeks. She didn't feel threatened by him, but the wretched sadness that crawled up her back made her glad she wasn't alone.

He handed her a handkerchief and looked away, giving her some privacy.

She blotted her face and then blew her nose, taking her time to evaluate him. Everything said that this man could be trusted. She took a breath and worked to lock down her feelings. It had been a long time since she'd been this out of control.

"I'm Joshua Lighthouse," he said as he sat next to her on the ground. He dug into his pack. He pulled out something wrapped in leather and offered it to her.

The food smelled of strange spices and it made her mouth water. How long had it been since she'd eaten? She took the food. "Thank you."

She took a bite and focused on the spice. Since she had failed her mission and didn't want to go back to Hope, she needed a place to stay and a job. "Is there a town nearby?"

She'd already decided that there must be. Joshua didn't look like a farmer or a huntsman.

"New Nadezhda is near." His brow furrowed, but he didn't ask her where she was from.

"What sort of skills do they value there?" she asked. Since she was one of the few non-magical people from Ho—her hometown. If this new town only valued magic, she could be in trouble.

He shrugged. "What are you good at?"

"I know Hapkido." Seeing his blank expression, she added, "It's a fighting style."

He nodded, looking thoughtful. "I could use some back-up on what I'm currently working on."

Rose evaluated his face. She'd always had a sense for knowing when people were lying. Joshua was not lying. He could use the help. She didn't have many options, and he had been kind. Perhaps she could prove she was more than a sobbing woman.

"What do we need to do?" she asked.

"There is a vampire near here who has been killing in the city. I'm here to persuade him to stop." Joshua said it calmly, like it was a normal day for him to walk into a vampire's lair.

She studied his expression and the way he held himself. He acted as if he believed vampires were real.

"Do vampires really exist?"

Joshua nodded. "They do."

She thought about everything she had seen and heard about the myth of vampires. "So, he's undead, and only a stake through the heart can stop him?"

"There are other ways, but that's the most reliable one. I also have this." He pulled out a vial. "This has holy water and other things and will harm the undead." He tucked the bottle back into his bag.

Even though he seemed to be telling the truth, she still thought he must be joking. There was no such thing as a vampire. Was there?

His face and everything about him supported his words. The shield had been put up to protect Hope hundreds of years ago. Could it have been used to prevent things like vampires from entering Hope? Was that what Hope's founders had seen, what caused them to put up a wall? Why hadn't New Nadezhda put up a shield?

"I'll go, but I have questions."

"Shoot." He led her along a path near the edge of the woods.

How else was this world like Hope? "Are there many mages in the city?"

"Some. Mages are relatively rare."

Hope was full of mages. She and Max had been two of only a handful of people without magic. "And are there many creatures like the vampire here?"

Joshua raised an eyebrow at her. "Yes, there are many types of undead. Most are not intelligent. Vampires are." His tone had stayed even, but something about the slight downward curve of his mouth made her think Joshua didn't like the undead.

"Are there other things?"

"All the creatures from Earth came into this world with the Merge." His face twisted as if he was remembering something unpleasant.

She followed Joshua, barely keeping track of where they were going.

The shield had protected Hope from the Merge. She would have to get used to many different creatures. She hadn't read much about fairytales. That had been more Max and her husband's thing. The ache of grief closed her throat for a moment. She forced the emotions away.

"We're here," Joshua whispered.

A small tower, perhaps two stories high, squatted in a clearing. It didn't seem to have any windows. But that made sense. Didn't vampires have an issue with the sun? The surrounding vegetation looked like it belonged in a fairytale, dark and twisted and full of thorns.

"One of the agents at the Human Protection Agency, the HPA, swears he got in a killing blow when he rescued the woman the vampire was trying to kill." He turned back to look at her. "Sorry, I had forgotten you were without a weapon." He handed her a long dagger.

She took it, did a practice swing, and assumed her first stance. The dagger was a few inches shorter than the sword she had trained with, but would work.

Joshua grinned at her. "Ready?"

She nodded.

At Joshua's touch, the door creaked open. The smell of decay tickled her nose.

Joshua lit a torch. The room seemed to be the full length of the tower. A staircase extended down into murky darkness and up to the next level.

The smell of decay was stronger up here. "Which way?" she whispered.

Joshua pointed down.

The first stirring of unease hit her. She knew what he was hunting was upstairs, but perhaps he had a reason to go down? She wasn't sure, so she kept quiet.

Rose crept behind him, trying to make no sound.

"Why are you with the human?" The voice in her head sounded male and old.

Her heart picked up speed. She'd never heard a voice in her head before.

Something pungent clogged her nose. The sense she and

Joshua were heading into a trap pressed on her chest. She grabbed Joshua's shoulder.

He stopped and glanced back. "What's wrong?"

"The vampire is upstairs..." She wasn't sure how to explain that going down was a trap or that she knew the vampire was upstairs. But she did. She was confident in her conclusions.

He glanced down for a moment. His breathing changed, and then all the color left his face. He took a shuddery breath. "Go back," he mouthed.

She went back up the stairs, and then Joshua led again, going up to the second floor.

The room was almost as dark as the room below, which made sense if there were no windows. It would be like a big cave.

A massive bed was just visible in the gloom. The decaying smell came from the bed.

Joshua lit a torch and brought it to the bed. The man who lay in the bed was desiccated. Dry skin stretched across his bones. A gaping wound lay open on his chest, but the wound didn't bleed.

"Lighthouse. Come to put me out of my misery?" the man hissed.

"If you agreed to not harm humans, I'd have no issue with you."

"You wish me to starve." The man leapt out of the bed, flying toward Joshua.

Joshua's first arrow hit the vampire in the throat, but the second went wide. It was enough. The vampire slowly disintegrated.

"*He will kill you, too, when he finds out.*" The old male voice reverberated in her head. It must have been the vampire.

The words in her head confused her. Why would Joshua kill her? She wasn't undead.

Eager for exclusive content? Want to be the first to know about upcoming releases and get a free short story?

Sign up for Claudia Blood's Newsletter at https://dl.bookfunnel.com/u5nf3wa84m

You can unsubscribe at any time.

BOOK OF SECRETS

Merged Worlds Series Book 1 - Book of Secrets

The human world and the world of myth have merged. Ordinary individuals must become extraordinary if they hope to save it.

Joshua Lighthouse never wanted to be a hero, but now, he has no choice.

For three hundred years, the human world and the world of Myth have lived as one. The cataclysmic Merge forced those who survived – both human and Others – to form factions.

As leader of the Human Protection Agency, Joshua is charged with maintaining the safety of the humans in his city. But he secretly protects an artifact more powerful than even he knows...

The Book of Secrets.

With the anniversary of the Merge approaching, the Book of Secrets is stolen and Joshua finds himself at the center of a plot to unmerge the worlds.

Stripped of his position, betrayed, and with a bounty on his head, Joshua must outrun the organization he once served and legions of Others in a race against time to locate the book and prevent the inter-species war that will end the world he knows forever.

Can he find his way to salvation when everything he believed is a lie, or will his distrust lead to another epic cataclysm he can't stop?

This is the first book in the Merged series. If you love urban fantasy stories full of desperate rescues, unexpected twists and tragic betrayals, you'll love this installment of Claudia Blood's epic series.

ACKNOWLEDGMENTS

Thanks to my hubby and family who allow me to wander away when I need to write.

To my VA Kelly I can't thank you enough for your undying enthusiasm and design sense. Social media is way less scary with you on my side.

To my amazing developmental editor Dawn Alexander who helped me organize my chaos and keep my inner achiever from getting too enthusiastic.

Thank you Fenley Grant for your amazing editing skills and for working me in when I am inevitably late.

Thank you Wendy for reading and giving feedback to my writing since college. (A scary number of years ago) You were always able to find a nugget of good that kept me going.

Thank you to the ladies at Lakehouse Writers group, Tammy, Val, MaryAnna, B, Jay, and Kim who have been a constant source of inspiration, motivation, and sanity checking.

Thank you to Val and MaryAnna who kept me honest on our accountability texts and for helping me figure out the end of this book. You both were so patient with my what-if-ing.

Thank you Antha and Christine for the many, many, many writing sprints. Without you guys I never would have gotten the book done.

Thank you to Calley for the daily checkins. Cookies!

ABOUT THE AUTHOR

Claudia Blood writes mystical realms and futuristic worlds, where underdogs defy authority, defeat demons, and discover their destined family amidst the chaos.

Her love of Epic Fantasies led her from life as a research scientist right into that of an award-winning author. With works such as the Renegades Rising, *Relic trilogy*, <u>Merged series</u>, and the<u>Supernatural Detective Agency</u>. <u>Claudia Blood</u>'s works cover a wide range of genres and themes that have captivated many.

Juggling her roles as a wife, mom, business analyst, and pet wrangler doesn't leave much free time, but what Claudia has is filled to the brim with creating sci-fi and fantasy novels set in worlds that may be slightly familiar and some that are totally unique and new. Taking inspiration from all kinds of media from *Dungeons & Dragons*, *The Dresden Files*, Alan Dean Foster, and so much more, Claudia Blood crafts stories that entice and keep the reader wondering what will happen next.

For her latest release, visit her at
<u>www.ClaudiaBlood.com</u>